WELCOME TO
PASSPORT TO READING
A beginning reader's ticket to a brand-new world!

Every book in this program is designed to build read-along and read-alone skills, level by level, through engaging and enriching stories. As the reader turns each page, he or she will become more confident with new vocabulary, sight words, and comprehension.

These PASSPORT TO READING levels will help you choose the perfect book for every reader.

READING TOGETHER
Read short words in simple sentence structures together to begin a reader's journey.

READING OUT LOUD
Encourage developing readers to sound out words in more complex stories with simple vocabulary.

READING INDEPENDENTLY
Newly independent readers gain confidence reading more complex sentences with higher word counts.

READY TO READ MORE
Readers prepare for chapter books with fewer illustrations and longer paragraphs.

This book features sight words from the educator-supported Dolch Sight Words List. This encourages the reader to recognize commonly used vocabulary words, increasing reading speed and fluency.

For more information, please visit passporttoreadingbooks.com.

Enjoy the journey!

Little, Brown and Company
Hachette Book Group
1290 Avenue of the Americas, New York, NY 10104
Visit us at LBYR.com
www.uglydolls.com

First Edition: April 2019

Little, Brown and Company is a division of Hachette Book Group, Inc.
The Little, Brown name and logo are trademarks of Hachette Book Group, Inc.

The publisher is not responsible for websites (or their content)
that are not owned by the publisher.

Library of Congress Control Number 2019930952

ISBNs: 978-0-316-42446-2 (pbk.), 978-0-316-42442-4 (ebook),
978-0-316-42445-5 (ebook), 978-0-316-42444-8 (ebook)

Printed in the United States of America

CW

10 9 8 7 6 5 4 3 2 1

Meet the

UGLY DOLLS

Adapted by Celeste Sisler

LITTLE, BROWN AND COMPANY
New York Boston

Attention, UglyDolls fans!
Look for these words when you read this book.
Can you spot them all?

reporter

party

leader

treats

Welcome to Uglyville!
Uglyville celebrates the
weird and the strange.
It is also the home of the
strange and weird UglyDolls.

Meet Moxy.
She is full of heart.
Moxy is good at making
her friends feel warm
and fuzzy.

Moxy is also a reporter.
She writes about
Uglyville every day.
Then she delivers her
newspaper all over
town with Ugly Dog.

Ugly Dog is Moxy's best friend. He is always ready to make the newest UglyDolls in town feel welcome.

Ugly Dog loves to
sing and rap.
He knows the best
song for any party.
Go, Ugly Dog!

Ox is the mayor of Uglyville.
He is a great leader and
a great friend, too!

Ox likes throwing fun parties!
He is sure to invite all
the UglyDolls in Uglyville.

Lucky Bat is very calm.
He helps the other UglyDolls
when they are worried.

Lucky Bat gives great advice
to all his friends.
But he is not always confident
because he cannot fly.
Lucky Bat hides the fact
that he tries to fly.

Wage loves baking.
Her friends enjoy
eating her yummy treats!

Wage has many hobbies.
She also loves art, video games,
and dressing up.

Babo is strong, kind,
and HUNGRY!
He is the hungriest of all
the UglyDolls in Uglyville.

Babo does not talk much,
but he loves to eat
Wage's desserts.

Every day the UglyDolls have a party with old and new friends. The UglyDolls love being Ugly!

But Moxy thinks things could be even better. She dreams of one day belonging to a child of her own.

Moxy is tired of waiting to be picked for the Big World— she decides that she will find her child herself!

Moxy tells her friends
that it is time to make
all their dreams come true.
They set off on an adventure!

They find a mysterious tunnel.
Where does it lead?

Inside the tunnel
is a giant slide.

The slide leads somewhere the UglyDolls have never been before.

INSTITUTE OF

It is called the Institute of Perfection.
What is this place?

The UglyDolls meet
the dolls of Perfection.

The Perfect Dolls do not
look like the UglyDolls.
They think the UglyDolls
are very weird!

The UglyDolls need to compete with the Perfect Dolls to make their dreams of going to the Big World come true.

It will be hard, but
they know that they
can rely on one another.

No matter what the Perfect Dolls think, the UglyDolls like being different. Being different makes them special!